Flash Plays Golf

By Charlie Alexander

Library of Congress Control Number: 2016911558

ISBN: Softcover   978-1-5245-2559-0
        Hardcover   978-1-5245-2560-6
        EBook   978-1-5245-2556-9

Print information available on the last page

Rev. date: 07/16/2016

To order additional copies of this book, contact:
Xlibris
1-888-795-4274
www.Xlibris.com
Orders@Xlibris.com

Flash Plays Golf

Written by Charlie Alexander

Art work by Charlie Alexander

Golf Tournament at the Villages of Florida

Arnold Palmer Country Club

Flash had his own set of golf clubs.

Charlie and Becky had them
custom made just for Flash!

"Is this the first tee?" asked Flash.

Flash was ready to play.

Flash needs a good shot!

"SWING AWAY Flash!"

Just stayed in bounds.

And a good shot through the trees!

Looks like Flash found the sand trap.

This might be a difficult shot!

Trapped in the sand bunker.

Flash thinks it's a good idea to keep
his mouth closed for this shot.

Flash didn't want to hit the ball in the water!

It was time for his best swing.

Over the water.

And onto the green. What a shot!

Flash thought he was in heaven after that shot!

He pictured himself with angel Wings.

Putt for doe!

Flash was hoping to make par!

At last! The windmill hole!

"Good luck Flash!"

"The clouds are rolling in fast." said Flash.

"The wind is picking up."

Flash was getting ready to report on the stormy weather.

"Lots of wind and rain." reported Flash.

"It's raining cats and dogs!"

Flash was hoping the weather would clear soon.

He was getting really hungry! And it was pouring rain anyway.

What a great time for lunch!

The sun was coming back out of the clouds.

And Flash was ready to play on.

Flash knew he needed a birdie to win!

He was happy to be playing so well!

"Try not to swing too fast Flash!"

The snail and the turtle chimed in.

"May I suggest a 7 iron?" croaked the alligator.

Flash thanked him for such good advice!

"Am I aimed ok?" asked Flash.

"A little more to the left." replied the frog and the alligator. "There's a lot of wind today!"

Flash liked driving
the golf cart.

And now the rain was letting up.

Flash could hardly believe all of his friends came.

They were cheering him on!

He could only dream of winning the trophy.

Flash was so excited!

His caddie said "Hop to it Flash!"

A good shot is needed now.

Focus!

This putt for the win

Flash will win if this putt goes in!

A Flash Victory!

Another great day!

It was beginning to get dark.

Luckily Flash was on his way to receive his trophy!

Flash felt like everyone was watching him.

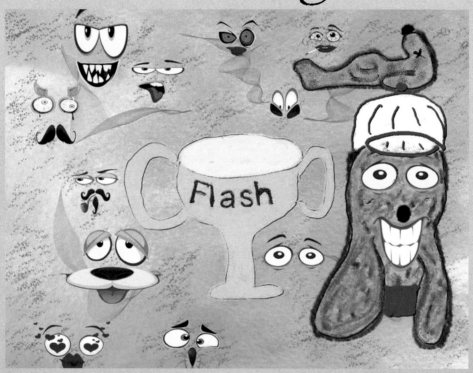

They were all happy about his glorious golf adventure.

Flash & Charlie were having their picture taken.

"Congratulations Flash! I'm so proud of you!" said Charlie.

Flash's trophy barely fit in the trunk. But it was the best ride home ever!

Charlie, Becky & Flash were happy together!

"Here we are Flash! We're home boy!" Charlie said happily.

Flash was grateful to be home with Charlie & Becky! (And a trophy too!)

The End

Printed in the United States
By Bookmasters